The Dark

The Dark

by Robert Munsch
illustrated by Michael Martchenko

Annick Press Ltd.
Toronto • New York

Annick Press gratefully acknowledges the support of the
Canada Council and the Ontario Arts Council.

Cataloguing in Publication Data

Munsch, Robert N., 1945-
        The dark

(Munsch for kids)
2nd rev. ed.
ISBN 1-55037-451-6 (bound)
ISBN 1-55037-450-8 (pbk.)

I. Martchenko, Michael. II. Title.
III. Series: Munsch, Robert N., 1945-   .
Munsch for kids.

PS8576.U575D37 1997   jC813'.54   C97-930905-0
PZ7.M86Da 1997

Distributed in Canada by:
Firefly Books Ltd.
3680 Victoria Park Avenue
Willowdale, ON
M2H 3K1

Published in the U.S.A. by Annick Press (U.S.) Ltd.
Distributed in the U.S.A. by:
Firefly Books (U.S.) Inc.
P.O. Box 1338
Ellicott Station
Buffalo, NY 14205

Printed and bound in Canada by
Kromar Printing Ltd.

To Jule Ann

When Jule Ann came down the stairs for breakfast, there was a big cookie jar on the kitchen table. She turned it upside down, but nothing came out.

So she hit the bottom of the jar, whap, whap, whap, whap; and still nothing came out. Finally she held the jar up over her head and looked in it.

A small dark lump fell out, bounced on her nose and rolled across the table.

Jule Ann said, "WHAT'S THAT!"

Her mother said, "WHAT'S THAT!"

The small dark ate Jule Ann's shadow and got a little bigger.

The small dark ate her mother's shadow and got a little bigger.

The small dark ate the toaster's shadow and got even bigger.

"I think it's a Dark," said Jule Ann. By this time the Dark was as big as the toaster.

Jule Ann's father came in and said, "HEY, WHAT'S THAT!"

Jule Ann said, "It's a Dark. It eats shadows."

Jule Ann's father picked up the Dark
and threw it out the window.

The Dark landed and bounced:
boing, boing, boing, down the street.

The Dark saw lots of car shadows and it ATE THEM UP.

The Dark saw lots of telephone pole shadows and it ATE THEM UP.

The Dark saw lots of house shadows and it ATE THEM UP.

The Dark even saw some butterfly shadows and it ATE THEM UP.

The Dark was now as big as a hill. It came back to Jule Ann's house, sat on the roof and went to sleep.

The whole yard was so dark that Jule Ann could not go out and play.

Jule Ann's mother and father said, "WHAT'S THIS!" They ran out to chase away the Dark.

But it was so dark outside that they got lost. They could not even find the door to come back in.

Jule Ann was very upset. Then she saw that the Dark had not eaten her chair's shadow; so she broke off a piece and held it out the window.

She yelled, "FOOD!" The Dark came right down the side of the house and jumped on the shadow.

Then Jule Ann broke up the rest of the shadow into little pieces and put them into the cookie jar.

Right away the Dark flew through the window and jumped into the jar to eat the shadow.

As soon as the Dark was inside, Jule Ann put the top on the jar. She taped it with tape. She glued it with glue. She plastered it with plaster and she roped it with rope.

Then all her friends helped her carry it to a garbage can and they dumped it inside. Her mother and father called the garbage truck. The truck came and took the Dark away. It never came back.

All the shadows took a whole week to grow again.

Other books in the Munsch for Kids series:

Mud Puddle
The Paper Bag Princess
The Boy in the Drawer
Jonathan Cleaned Up, Then He Heard a Sound
Murmel Murmel Murmel
Millicent and the Wind
Mortimer
The Fire Station
Angela's Airplane
David's Father
Thomas' Snowsuit
50 Below Zero
I Have to Go!
Moira's Birthday
A Promise is a Promise
Pigs
Something Good
Show and Tell
Purple, Green and Yellow
Wait and See
Where is Gah-Ning?
From Far Away
Stephanie's Ponytail

Many Munsch titles are available in French and/or
Spanish. Please contact your favourite supplier.